AN ORIGINAL TEDDY BEAR GOLDENDOODLE BOOK

FLETCHER

THE VERY FIRST
ENGLISH TEDDY BEAR
GOLDENDOODLE

written by
SHERRI SMERAGLIA

illustrated by
MEREDITH JOHNSON

Published by
Smeraglia Farm
SMERAGLIA ENTERPRISES, INC.

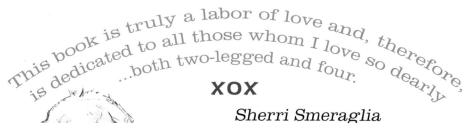

This book is truly a labor of love and, therefore, is dedicated to all those whom I love so dearly ...both two-legged and four.

XOX

Sherri Smeraglia

FLETCHER

The Very First English Teddy Bear Goldendoodle

Fletcher - The Very First English Teddy Bear Goldendoodle / by Sherri Smeraglia
Illustrated by Meredith Johnson
Book Design, Title Design and Production by Cathe Physioc
Title font: Pupcat / Text font: Clarendon

Summary: A family, an English Golden Retriever and a Standard Poodle get together to raise the very first Teddybear Goldendoodle on a farm in Alabama.

ISBN 978-0-9896192-0-2

Published by
Smeraglia Farm
Smeraglia Enterprises, Inc.
Robertsdale, Alabama U.S.A.

www.smeraglia.com
www.teddybeargoldendoodles.com

Hello!

My name is **FLETCHER.**

My mother and father are two very special dogs.
I'd like to share their story with you: how they met and,
of course, the most important part, how I became
the very first English Teddy Bear Goldendoodle.

Oh, I forgot to mention...
the cutest and most clever one of all!

It all began on a farm...
The Smeraglia Farm.
(SMER-AL-YUH)
My father, an English Golden Retricver,
was imported from Europe to be a companion
for the farm owners' five children. They named him
MUrphy.

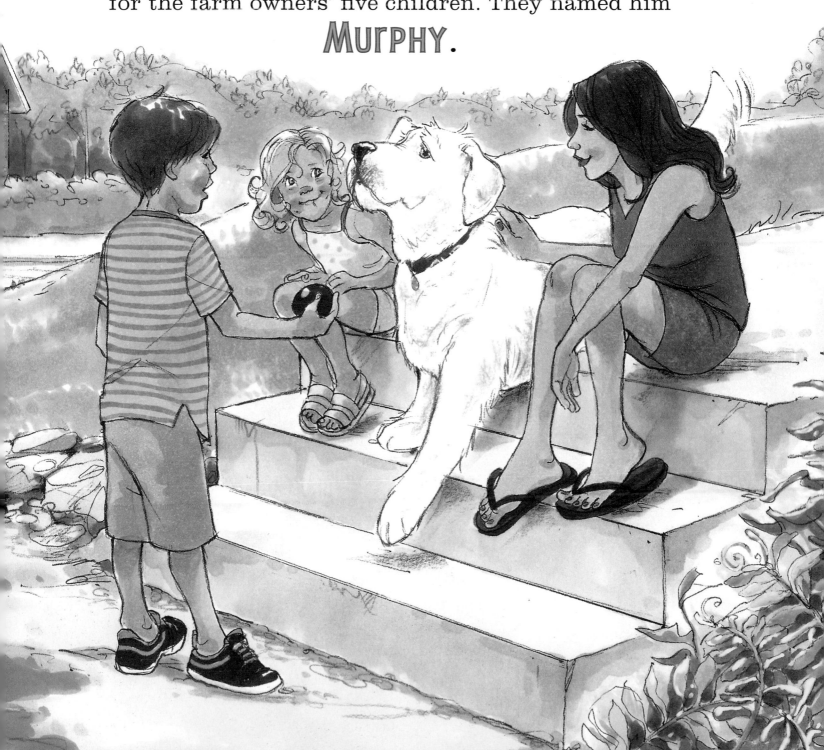

Murphy loved playing sports, hunted like an expert,
and retrieved anything from the bottom
of their great big swimming pool.

The Smeraglia boys and girls were always protected by him.

Every night before bedtime,
he would wander from bed to bed exchanging
wet, sloppy kisses for his most favorite treat of all...
BELLY RUBS!

One day everything suddenly changed.
The Smeraglias discovered that their youngest child,
Natalie, was very allergic to dog hair.

AH·CHOO

She coughed and sneezed and her eyes constantly
watered and itched. No matter how many times they
vacuumed Murphy's hair, Natalie stayed sick.

Mr. & Mrs. Smeraglia decided to build Murphy
his very own house right next to theirs,
until they could come up with a better solution.
It looked just like a castle, suited for a king.

They furnished it with everything an
English Golden Retriever would want, including a
king-size bed, topped with a cozy down comforter.

Murphy loved his new home, but he was also sad.
At night he knew he would no longer snuggle and cuddle
with the Smeraglia children or fall asleep to his
favorite thing in the whole wide world... BELLY RUBS!

The next part of this story is my favorite...

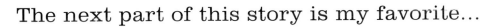

One day, family friends of the Smeraglias stopped by with the most **beautiful standard poodle** Murphy had ever seen.

Her name was **Georgette**.

She didn't know it yet, but she was going to be my mother. Georgette looked just like a real princess. She was as white as snow with tight curls that must have taken hours to twist and twirl. She had sparkly, pink pawnails, and each leg had a perfectly round pom pom just above her foot.

When Murphy returned from
hunting with the boys,
Lukas, Jacob and Joe,
he caught sight of this
beauty and could do nothing
but
pant
and
drool.

Mr. Smeraglia gently stroked the top of
Murphy's head and calmly said,
"Settle down, good boy, settle down."

Everybody (except for Georgette) believed Murphy
was acting strangely because he was
overheated from a hard day's work.

Georgette thought Murphy was extremely handsome
and blushed from all the attention he showed to her.

Georgette's owners became missionaries and decided
to travel around the world. They couldn't think of
a better home for Georgette than the Smeraglia Farm.
At first, Georgette was sad.
She was going to miss her owners.
But, the Smeraglia family made her feel right at home.

Murphy didn't mind that she was allowed to sleep
with the children, because he thought she was
a princess and needed **lots** of BELLY RUBS!

When Mr. & Mrs. Smeraglia noticed that Georgette
didn't shed and that Natalie didn't get sick,
they thought of a great plan.

(I'm not exactly sure what that plan was, but I think it had
something to do with me and my brothers and sisters.)

Natalie's older sister, Lauren, is very talented.
She can put someone in a spinning chair
and they end up looking like a movie star.

(Georgette loves getting dolled up in the Powder Room
while Lauren makes her gorgeous.)

Whenever she was finished being groomed,
Georgette would race to the courtyard where Murphy
was always waiting to give her a wet, sloppy kiss.

Georgette and Murphy grew very fond of one another and spent most of their days swimming with the children,

learning new tricks,

and chasing butterflies
along the edge of the flower garden.

Georgette and Murphy had fallen in love.

Natalie noticed how much they cared for one another
and insisted they get married.

She planned a sweet little wedding and picked
at least one hundred roses from their rose garden
and placed them all about in the courtyard.
Natalie invited all the neighborhood friends and family,
and the farm horses and dogs, too.

In place of wedding rings, Natalie tied a pink bow around
Georgette's neck and a blue bow around Murphy's neck.

Everybody who attended this grandiose event laughed
and cheered as the new Mr. and Mrs. Murphy Smeraglia
pranced around the courtyard eating
the most delicious treats they had ever tasted.

For a wedding gift, Natalie prepared a beautiful bed,
fit for a queen, and put it beside Murphy's.

Now the rest of this story is about me,

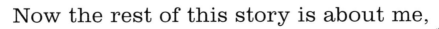

FLETCHER...

The most clever pup EVER!

The following Christmas, before the sun came up,
Georgette had the most wonderful
gift for the Smeraglia family.

Mr. and Mrs. Smeraglia couldn't believe their eyes.

My mother had given birth to seven little girls

and seven little boys.

I was the first one born.

They tied a blue satin bow around my neck
and placed me under their
Christmas tree on top of a box
wrapped with snowman paper.

When the Smcraglia boys ran into the room
to see what was under the tree for them,
they didn't even noticc me.

They thought I was a toy teddy bear
until Natalie squealed with delight saying,
"Momma! It's a real live Teddy Bear!
Where ever did you find one?"

Natalie cuddled me in her arms and said,

"I shall call you... FLETCHER!
We will be best friends."

Everybody in the neighborhood came to take a peek at me
and my thirteen brothers and sisters that Christmas day.
All we kept hearing was how we looked exactly like
teddy bears. And, so, the Smeraglias started calling us
their precious Teddy Bear Goldendoodles.

I still don't know what a teddy bear is,
but I'm sure it's adorable, just like me.

We look a little like our father - soft and cuddly;
and a little bit like our mother - big, beautiful eyes
and wavy hair that doesn't shed.

We're a perfect combination of the two.

As I got a little bit older and began to toddle out,
Natalie started sneaking me into her bed at night.

Mrs. Smeraglia made the softest toy puppy
in the whole world for Natalie and me.

We both loved to cuddle and snuggle with it.

When Natalie's Momma tucked her in,
she thought I was one of Natalie's favorite teddy bears
until I rolled over for a quick
BELLY RUB!

Natalie and her Momma would giggle and laugh until
Mr. Smeraglia would holler from the bedroom down the hall,
"Okay, girls! Save it for morning. It's bedtime."

When Natalie returned from school in the afternoons,
she would teach me really cool tricks.

I could roll over... three times in a row.

I could sit and give
her five with one paw,
then ten with the other.

I learned how to retrieve just about anything,
even the newspaper for Mr. Smeraglia.

One day, Natalie's favorite doll fell in their
swimming pool and I even retrieved her.

I learned to help Natalie find her way in the dark
when we visited the horses in the barn.

She even taught me how to bark different ways
when I needed to speak to her.

When the Smeraglias discovered how smart their
Teddybear Goldendoodles were, they decided to share us with
the rest of the world. They knew there were thousands of
wonderful families who could use such helping dogs,
especially ones that don't make people sneeze.

So, this is my story...
that explains how I, FLETCHER, became
the very first English Teddy Bear Goldendoodle
and the most extraordinary one of all.
Not only am I adorable, but I'm also very gifted.
Rumor has it, I may be a genius.
There is *one thing* I am working on...
that's turning my little licks into great, big sloppy kisses
in exchange for those amazing BELLY RUBS!

THE END

HUGS & BELLY RUBS

XOX